P9-CMR-425

For my two young friends Faye and Marie, who live in Egypt —D.H.
For my brother, Andrew —J.D.

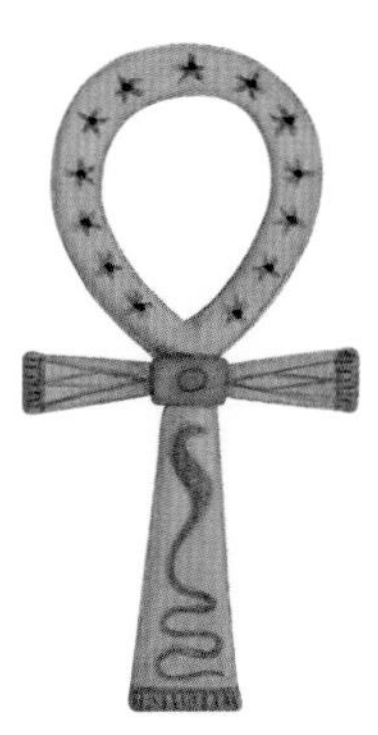

With thanks to the Department of Egyptian Antiquities at The British Museum

By arrangement with The Inkman, Cape Town, South Africa
Hand-lettering by Andrew van der Merwe

Printed in Hong Kong
First published in Great Britain by Frances Lincoln Limited, 2001
First American edition, 2001
1 3 5 7 9 10 8 6 4 2

Library of Congress Cataloging-in-Publication Data
Hofmeyr, Dianne.
The star-bearer : a creation myth from Ancient Egypt / Dianne Hofmeyr ; pictures by Jude Daly.— 1st American ed.
p. cm.
ISBN 0-374-37181-4
1. Mythology, Egyptian—Juvenile literature. 2. Creation—Juvenile literature. [1. Mythology, Egyptian. 2. Creation.]
I. Daly, Jude, ill. II. Title.

BL2450.C74 H64 2001
299'.31—dc21 00-37586

The Star-Bearer

A Creation Myth from Ancient Egypt

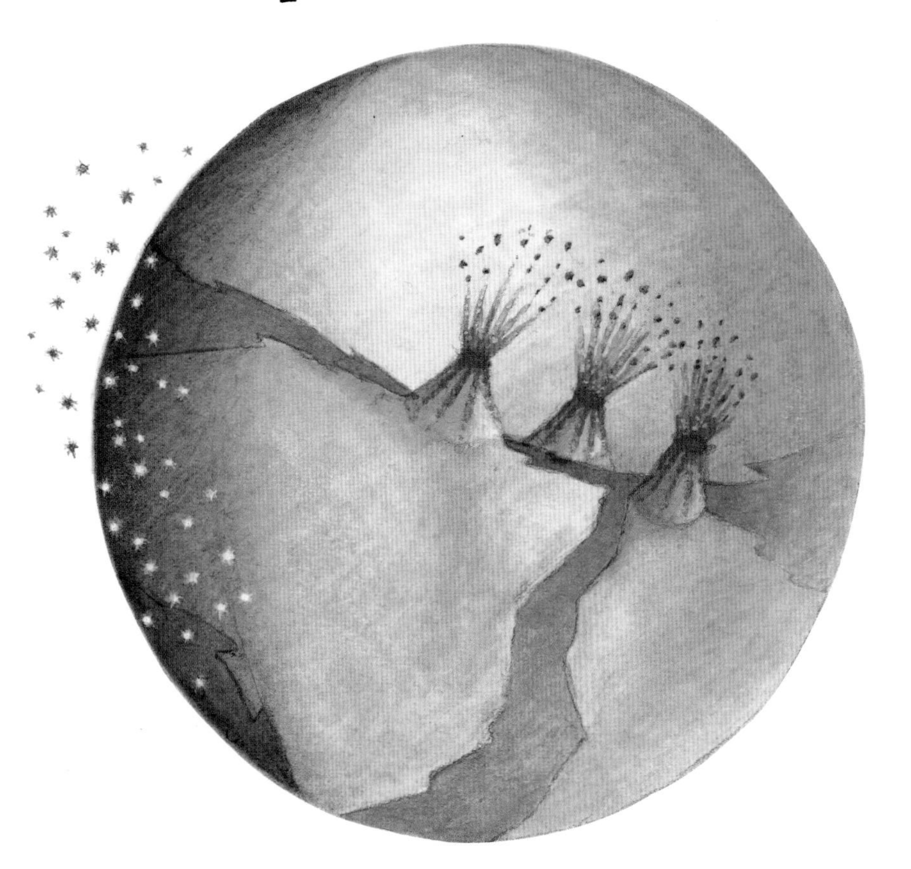

Dianne Hofmeyr & Jude Daly

FARRAR STRAUS GIROUX • NEW YORK

Three distinct groups of ancient Egyptian myths stem from the cities of Heliopolis, Hermopolis, and Memphis. The stories are often inconsistent, even within one group. This story is based on the Heliopolis creation myth. Accounts of the myth can be found in the oldest literature in the world, the Pyramid Texts, dating from 3000 B.C., which were preserved in the royal pyramids of the Fifth and Sixth Dynasties. The myth is also to be found in the later Coffin Texts and the Book of the Dead, dating from the Twelfth and Thirteenth Dynasties.

Pronunciation guide

Atum – *AH-tum*
Geb – *GEB* ("*g*" as in "*get*")
Horus – *HOR-us*
Isis – *EYE-sis*
Khonsu – *KON-soo*
Nephthys – *NEF-thys*
Nut – *NOOT*
Osiris – *Oh-SAI-ris*
Set – *SET*
Shu – *SHOO*
Tefnut – *TEF-noot*
Thoth – *THOTH* (rhymes with "*both*")

In the beginning, there was nothing but darkness and water that lay cold and still as black marble. Nothing moved in the inky silence.

After countless ages, a ripple formed beneath the black water and the bud of a lotus flower pushed upward. As the petals slowly unfurled, they spread a blue luster in the darkness. Enclosed in the center of the bloom was the golden godchild Atum.

Atum stood up and cast the first gleam of brilliant light into the world. But before he could take pleasure in the splendor, the flower pulled him back into its heart and sank into the dark depths.

This happened again and again. Atum grew lonely with nothing but dark and light to keep him company. He longed for friends. So he blew across the surface of his hands in all directions: "*Shu . . . shu . . . shu . . .*" Gusts of air swirled around him and then swept away across the watery waste—this was Shu, the god of air.

Atum tried even harder. He blew over his hands again. "*Tff . . . Tff . . . Tff . . .*"
Drops of moisture flew in all directions—this was Tefnut, the goddess of dew and rain.

Shu and Tefnut loved to tease and play.

They raced about in wide circles, chasing each other over the surface of the water.

Shu blew up windstorms that drew the water into waves.

Tefnut threw down rain that beat it flat again.

Shu was blustery, and rasped and pounded. Tefnut was often tearful. She drizzled and drenched and spouted.

Together they were unrestrained, unpredictable, and tempestuous.

Shu and Tefnut had two children. Their son, Geb, the god of the earth, grew up green as jade with all the rain his mother showered on him. And their daughter, Nut, the goddess of the sky, grew up pure as aquamarine with all the love her father wrapped around her.

Geb and Nut were quieter than their parents. They clasped each other and laughed and whispered secrets in each other's ears. Sky clung to earth and earth to sky. They were inseparable.

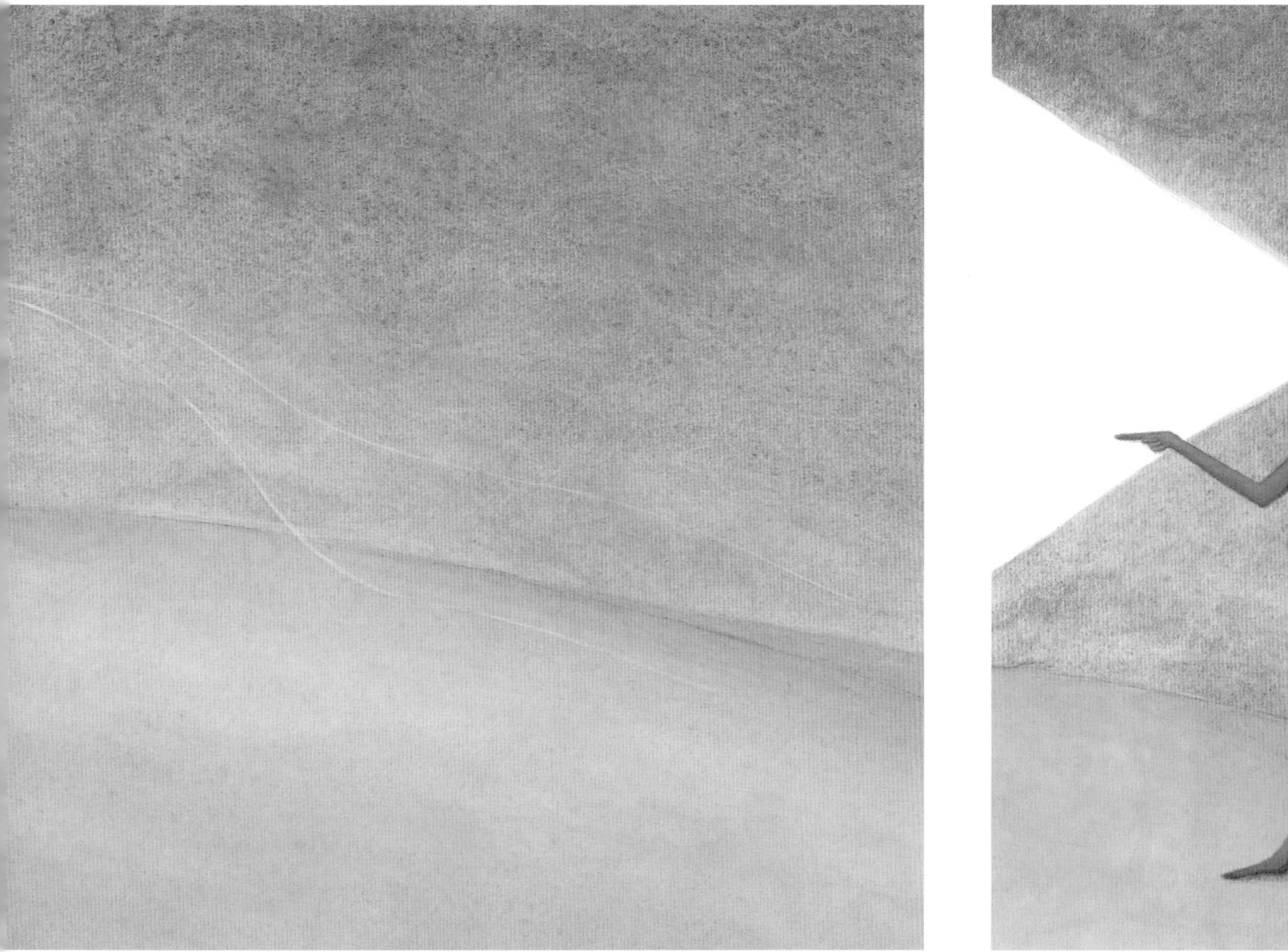

Atum the creator was upset. "I have work to do. I need space for my creation. If you stay so close to each other, there will be no room for tall trees and rugged mountains, for rivers and waterfalls and creatures with tall legs and long necks!"

But Geb and Nut paid no attention. They went on laughing and whispering secrets to each other.

Eventually Atum grew impatient and summoned Shu, their father.

"Separate your children," he commanded, "so that I can create the world and prevent the dark, watery wastes from returning."

Shu had to obey. He crawled between his son and daughter. Then he levered Nut upward, as if he were raising a tent of blue, and held Geb down firmly under his feet.

Geb struggled to free himself. His growls sent the first earthquakes shuddering through the land, and he spewed out the first volcanoes in anger. His mother, Tefnut, rushed to calm him with her soothing breath of rain, and her tears fell on the earth and grew into sweet-smelling plants.

Shu lifted Nut, his daughter, even higher until she arched in a silent vault over Geb, with her toes poised on the eastern rim of the world and her outstretched fingertips on the western rim. Geb strained upward in an attempt to reach out to her. But Shu kept him firmly in place.

As Geb lay gazing up at Nut, his outline turned into the craggy mountains and valleys of the earth's crust. And his mother's tears flowed into rivers and gathered in lakes around him.

Then Atum the creator took pity on Geb as he lay so still and separate, staring up at Nut. Atum created thousands and thousands of stars and sprinkled them over the length of Nut's body.

"There, Geb! Now you can see Nut in the darkness."

At last Atum had room to create whatever he desired. He scattered Nut's body with planets and a moon disk. Then he decorated Geb's dark skin with birds and beasts and plants.

He called out the names of gods to rule over them, and immediately the gods appeared—gods of love, wisdom, and justice.

Then Atum turned to Nut. "No child of *yours* shall spoil my creation or take my throne from me. I forbid *you* to give birth to a child on any day of the *year!*"

But something else happened. Thoth, the god of all wisdom, took pity on silent and beautiful Nut. He saw how lonely she was.

"You *shall* have children," he whispered. "I will find extra days in the year for you to have them."

So Thoth visited Khonsu, the god of the moon. He drew squares on a slate and challenged Khonsu to a game of checkers played with light and dark moonstones.

Every time Thoth placed a dark stone over one of Khonsu's light stones, Khonsu had to give up some light. Thoth managed to win five extra days of light for Nut to give birth.

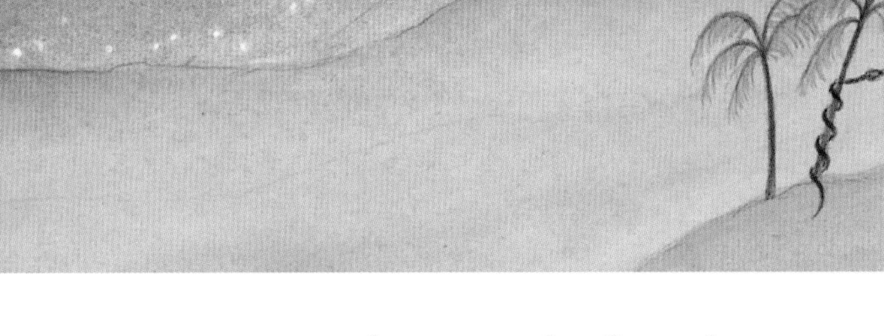

Osiris was born on the first day,

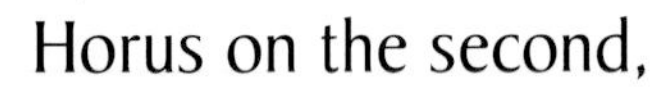

Horus on the second,

Set on the third,

Isis on the fourth, and Nephthys on the fifth.

And since that time the moon
has never been as bright or
as round as the sun.

After an eternity, Atum the creator grew old and tired. His bones turned to silver and his flesh to gold. He watched Nut's firstborn son, Osiris, grow tall and strong, and his heart softened. "Osiris shall have my throne!" he announced. "I will retire to the heavens."

So Nut took Atum in her arms and lifted him up into the heavens.

Now at last Nut is content. She gathers the golden disk of Atum in the east each morning and guides his journey across the sky. Then she gently lowers him in the west each evening.

On some days, she is crystal-clear aquamarine. On others, she is milky-white moonstone or opaque as turquoise.

Sometimes she has the luster of opal, at other times the brilliance of sapphire. Occasionally she is the deep, dark blue of lapis lazuli. And always at night, she enfolds the dark onyx sky against her star-studded bosom.

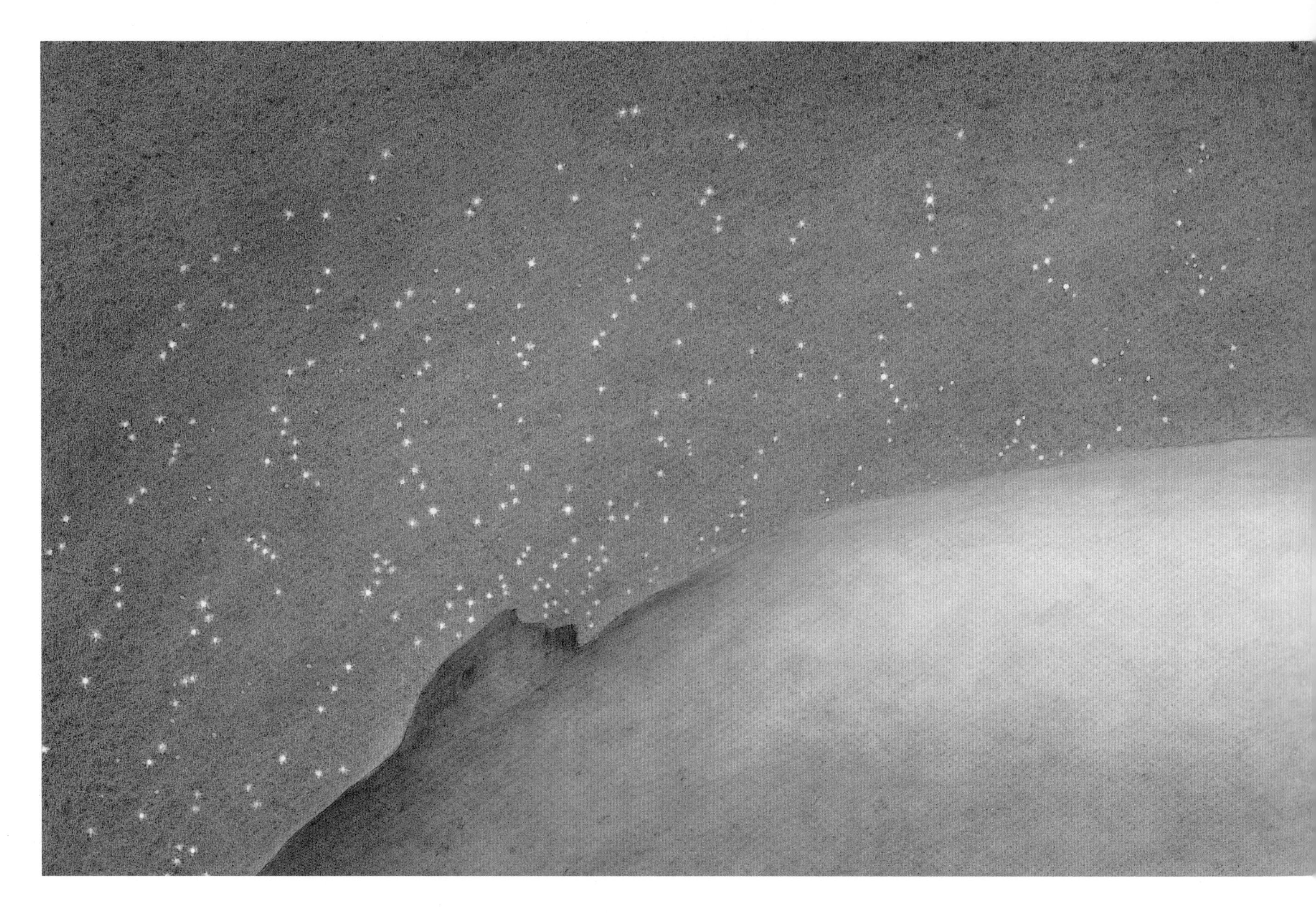

Now Geb lies silently gazing at Nut, enchanted by all her moods. Sometimes Shu's arms grow tired of holding Nut's body with its weight of stars. Then Nut leans down and tells secrets to her old love, Geb.

On these nights, the stars seem especially bright and close to the earth, and Nut's whispers float down softly as stardust.